MERRY IN SPITE

A FRIENDS-TO-LOVERS MM HOLIDAY ROMANTIC COMEDY

IRENE BAHRD

For anyone who wishes Hallmark movies were open-door...

Enjoy Chapters 2, 3, 4, 7, and 9.

CONTENT WARNINGS

Merry in Spite takes place in fictional Coal's Lake, Alberta. Since they are in Canada, both POVs are written with extra u's in words that wouldn't have them in the US.

By reading this book, there is a good chance you will experience the following side effects:

- Falling in love with a fictional man... or two.
- Craving an eggnog latte.
- Hooking up with your significant other in a bookstore.
- Contacting your high school best friend you had a crush on. *(Don't do this.)*
- Adopting a goldendoodle. *(Don't be impulsive. This probably isn't the best idea, either.)*
- Ordering a 5-gallon bucket of lube. *(Yes, it exists. Do not add to cart... or do. I'm not your mom.)*
- Adding a bunch of MM romance to your TBR.

You're welcome.

All jokes aside, this is a fast-burn ErotiCom (**high-spice romantic comedy**) with a ton of on-page explicit content. It is intended for mature audiences. Also, it's a short novella, so only expect this sexy read to make you break out your buzzbuzz a few times before it's over.

Additionally, there are scenes with:

- MM — two hot guys getting it on
- Oral sexytime — it's an Irene Bahrd trademark, you knew it was coming, even with two dudes
- Cliché hockey romance — he's retired, but still
- Piercings — Myles has a Jacob's Ladder
- Butt stuff — lots and lots of butt stuff

Ok, fine, this is a shopping list and not warnings...

If you are triggered by anything in this book, do us both a favor and don't read anything else in my backlist. Even though this is one of the spiciest stories I've told, the rest of my books are equally unhinged.

Author Note: This is NOT a how-to guide. You will probably be arrested if caught fucking in public. Also, there are NO conversations about protection from STIs in this book. Please be safe and talk to your doctor about what works best for you and/or your sexual partners.

PROLOGUE

MYLES

"Mr. Comet, I have... um... er... the *other* Mr. Comet on line four."

"Thank you, Cathy," I growl through clenched teeth at my assistant, gripping the armrest of my chair at the mention of my father.

While most days Cathy's presence brings me serenity, today it doesn't. My blood is boiling and I'm losing my composure. I crack my neck, roll my shoulders, and take a long breath before answering.

He beats me to a greeting, "Myles. So glad that perky assistant of yours was helpful today." I mute the phone and groan as he continues, "Your mother and I would like you at the lake for Christmas this year."

No. Absolutely not. There's no way in hell I'm going home for the holidays. I'd rather be diced up and thrown into a pressure cooker to be turned into stew than show up in Coal's Lake this year.

I reluctantly press 'unmute.'

"I have plans," I reply.

"At home with us? Fantastic, I'll let her know you're coming. I know that money's gone to your head. Perhaps a few weeks here will turn you back into the man I raised you to be."

Fuck. Here we go...

I left Coal's Lake seven years ago. It's been seven blissful years away from the nosy neighbors, overzealous matchmakers, and... Tristan Anderson, the captain of the hockey team—who only saw me as a friend.

I spent the first twenty years of my life living in a small town, annoyed as fuck. I sure as hell don't want to go back to some sort of cliché, made-for-TV-movie montage for Christmas. I know my parents will have all sorts of shit planned for me if I show up.

I paid my dues. I got out. The end.

"No, I already told you I'm busy."

"Myles David Comet. I did not put up with your shi—*nanigans* for the last few decades for you to miss another holiday. Your mother insists," my father spits. The angrier he gets, the grittier his thick Canadian accent becomes.

Mine only comes out after too much cinnamon whiskey or when talking to Pops. I mask it most days, since the last thing I need to hear on a call is someone throwing out a mocking 'eh?' or making yet another Tim Hortons joke while on a call with London or Sydney.

I sigh. "Four days, that's all I can do."

"You'll miss the tree lighting. Come on the first and stay for a month."

I know the desperation in his voice is a trap, but I counter, "Five."

"Two weeks."

"One. December 20-26th. Final offer."

He laughs, and while I miss hearing his levity, I remain resolute as he replies, "You think you can have a proper Christmas here in less than a week? Tristan doesn't even have his big holiday party until New Year's Eve."

My heart stops. Tristan is still there? It can't be the same Tristan; it has to be a different guy. Last I heard, he'd gone pro and was playing for an American hockey team on the east coast.

"New Years?" I can't help the hope blanketing my voice.

"I thought that might get your attention," he snickers. "I'll see you on the first." He hangs up without another word.

Fuck.

In less than five minutes, my life's been upended—going from ritual and routine, to chaos smothered in tinsel and fruitcake. May as well throw in a poinsettia to ensure it's culturally diverse. Spoiler: it's not.

IRENE BAHRD

Why is Tristan back?

TRISTAN

DECEMBER 1ST

I've been pacing my living room for the past two hours. Why is he here? And for a fucking month? The last thing I need is my high school crush showing up after seven years.

After helping Levi unbox his latest shipment at the bookstore, I should feel lighter. Venting to him usually helps; we both had injuries that ended our hockey careers, so he understands me better than most other people here in town. Instead, I still have to figure out how the hell I'm going to avoid Myles until he leaves after New Years.

I had to do a double take this morning when I saw him getting out of his pop's pickup. He looks like a completely different man than I remember, with his perfectly trimmed beard, expertly-fitted charcoal gray suit, and leather shoes that probably cost more than a down payment on a home around here.

Myles' parents moved next door to mine five years ago. It didn't phase me, since Myles hasn't returned to Coal's Lake since high school. I left as quickly as he did, returning two years ago after my injury; my knees were never the same after a pair of surgeries. Though, with how my heart stopped and cock twitched when I saw Myles, I'd have no issue being on my knees for him.

Fuck. What am I saying? He doesn't see me that way, and I shouldn't be fantasizing about a guy I haven't spoken to in years. I tilt my head, cracking my neck, and shake away the thought of a hookup that will never happen. No matter how much I tried to get his attention, he never saw me as more than a friend.

When we were younger, Myles always had his nose in a book, while I spent most of my time on the ice trying to stay out of the sin-bin... but failing. My temper always seemed to get the best of me. Retiring from hockey and moving back home definitely mellowed me out.

Growing up together, we spent summers on the lake and winters on the ice. Our families even vacationed together a few times. We were inseparable. Our moms were practically planning our wedding when we both came out the summer we turned 15. I'd secretly hoped he liked me, since I was crushing hard on him for at least two years. Instead, he retreated that Christmas and our friendship fell apart before I had a chance to tell him how I felt about him.

Blowing on my hot eggnog latte as I'm leaving The Reindeer Cafe, I turn the corner without looking and accidentally collide with someone walking in. My drink splashes between us, coating my leather jacket and their dark gray wool trench coat.

"Sorry, didn't see you there." I begin pointlessly wiping the hot drink from our coats with my hand. "Let me—"

"It's fine."

Hearing his voice, I freeze and finally look up, finding familiar caramel brown eyes staring back at me. The world stops and I can't breathe. Nothing could've prepared me for seeing him after all these years. "Myles. Hi, sorry, let me grab napkins inside." I turn and toss my latte in the trash.

About to open the door, Myles beats me to it. "I said it's fine, really." A small smile tugs at his lips. Even if these are the most words we've spoken since we were kids, it's as if no time has passed. There's a comfortability between us I didn't expect. I grab a wad of napkins and begin swiping at our jackets, sopping up the remainder of my drink.

"Please let me pay for your dry cleaning," I offer.

He grips my wrist mid-wipe and my eyes meet his. "Tristan," he says softly. My breath catches and I would give anything to hear my name from his lips again. I didn't think I would feel this way so many years later. Yet, here I am, still way too into my high school crush. "Don't worry about it. It's just a coat." He releases my wrist and shrugs it off, folding it over his arm. "I was on my phone and wasn't looking where I was going."

I glance down at his hands, which at no point have occupied a phone. "Alright. Will you at least let me buy you a coffee?"

Shit, did that sound like I was asking him out?

"Everything ok over there?" Helen asks from behind the counter. Both of our eyes snap to her.

I clear my throat, throw away the napkins, and stuff my hands in my pockets. "Oh, sure."

"Was there something wrong with your latte? Let me make you a new one." She begins steaming the milk for my drink before I can protest.

"Would you mind making that two?" Myles asks and approaches the register. He retrieves forty dollars from his wallet and sets it on the counter. I remain rooted in place, willing my heart to stop getting ideas. "Keep the change."

Helen and I both are confused by the generous tip. I should explain to him that Helen never charges me, but I'm already so embarrassed by the last five minutes that I don't want to pile on any additional humiliation.

"So, what are we drinking?" he asks me when I join him to wait for our drinks.

"Eggnog lattes," Helen answers for me, attempting to conceal her smile. "Since you two are staying"—she gives me a knowing look—"why don't you have a seat and I'll bring them over with a couple of croissant sandwiches."

"Sorry, Helly, I'm not staying," I insist, clenching my jaw.

"Oh, right," Myles says carefully. I can feel the disappointment coming from him, the negative energy now consuming me. I don't have to look at Myles to know his face fell at my words.

"You're staying, Tris," Helen chimes in, glaring at me.

I lift my hands in surrender. "Ok, I'm staying," I laugh.

She then addresses Myles, "You, too."

"I can't stay, I have a few errands to run for my mom," he replies to Helen, then asks me, "Could you join me? It's been a long time since I've been here, I don't know where to find half the things on my list."

Myles pulls out a list of items that can be found at various shops around town—shops that have been open since before either of us were born. There's no way he's forgotten where to find the hardware store, florist, or bakery. He's so full of shit.

Helen peeks over to see his list as Neil approaches, bringing two wrapped croissant sandwiches. "Tris better help you with that list. Finding the only bakery in town is quite the scavenger hunt," she teases.

"Helly," I grit out.

Neil adds, "Why not take home a few of our scones to your mom? The lemon blueberry ones are her favourite. It'll save you a trip." I hadn't noticed it before but Neil hasn't taken his eyes off Helen. By the way she's blushing, I'd gather these two won't be just coworkers for much longer.

"I'll pack up four for each of you." Helen rushes off and Myles tries to stifle a laugh, likely noticing the same tension I am.

Myles leans in to whisper, "I know where the florist is, but I'd still like you to come."

Like a fucking teenage boy, my mind goes straight into the gutter. I shake away the thought. "Sure. My truck is parked down by The Book Nook, if you don't mind the walk."

"Not at all."

MYLES

I nervously adjust my dairy-soaked jacket. When he ordered his second latte, I stupidly ordered the same, leaving out that I haven't had anything resembling milk—let alone eggnog—in over five years. I shouldn't be so anxious around him, especially after all this time, but I can't help it. Seven years away from Coal's Lake, away from him, will do that.

Tristan's about to open the door for me to walk through, but I get it first. He nods as he passes the threshold, but a woman with a stroller is attempting to enter so I keep it open for them. I take a step to leave and an older gentleman approaches. Still, I hold the door; my mother would disown me if I even considered going first.

Eleven. Eleven other people entered and exited the cafe before I can finally walk through the door I've been holding.

"You can take the man out of Coal's but you can't take Coal's out of the man," Tristan teases from where he's been waiting for me.

I roll my eyes. "If it ever got back to my family, well, you know how it is."

"Are you staying at Jamie's?" he asks. The question confuses me. Jamie's Lodge is great, but I would never stay there while visiting my parents, even if it's been over half a decade.

There's also the matter of him seeing me this morning from my parent's house. At least, I think he saw me.

I sure as fuck saw him.

"No, I'm staying at my parents' place. I, uh, didn't expect to see you here. I thought you left?"

Tristan gestures for us to walk toward the bookstore. After a few steps, he explains he was injured and it ruined his professional hockey career. He's been teaching at the local high school ever since and helping out around town where needed.

"Mind if we head inside for a minute?" Tristan gestures to the bookshop. "I need to make sure Levi is all set with his last shipment." So much has changed since I was here last, half of these stores weren't here.

"Sure, I don't have anywhere I need to be," I say with a shrug.

I have four hundred places I need to be. Spending time with someone I pined after when I was younger doesn't even make the top ten of things I need to accomplish today. So, why am I throwing away my errand list, and heading into the local bookstore for a man who wouldn't look twice at me when we were teens?

Contemplating leaving my eggnog laden coat in his truck, I think better of it. The last thing he needs is the smell lingering for a month. Instead, I open the door for him, and six other patrons leaving. I'm not normally this polite, but Coal's seems to have changed a small piece of me, regardless of how long I've been away.

Or maybe it's because of Tristan...

We head inside and I expect rustling in the back, bookworms... or literally any sound. It's the most quiet I've experienced since arriving back in town.

Tristan walks further into the store between floor to ceiling rows of bookshelves. "Levi?" he calls out, but there's no response. Tristan turns back suddenly and we crash into one another. "Sorry, I didn't mean to—"

Instinctively, I press a finger to his lips to silence his apology. He's too fucking polite for his own good. I pull my hand away, instantly missing the feel of his lips on my fingertip. I clear my throat, shaking away the thought. "Stop apologizing," I insist. "It was an accident."

"You being here isn't an accident, Myles. You haven't been back in Coal's in over half a decade. Why are you here?"

You, I want to shout at the top of my lungs. Instead, I opt for the cowardly response of, "My family."

"Right." He nods but his obvious disappointment fills me with guilt for lying to him; I'm only here for Tristan. He looks away in thought for a moment and mutters, "Fuck it," under his breath before he takes my face in his hands and kisses me.

My soul escapes my fucking body. The one person I've wanted for years is kissing me in a dark corner of a bookstore—living every avid reader's fantasy. I must be dreaming, and in a few moments, someone will shake me awake.

Wanting to prolong my hallucination, I press him against the shelves behind him, books slipping off and clattering to the floor. While I feel mild embarrassment about the mess, I can't stop kissing him. Worse, I'm half-tempted to reach between us to see if I have the same effect on him as he has on me. As much as I dislike eggnog, I'd gladly taste it from his soft lips anytime.

"Tris, is that you?" a voice calls out.

I push away from Tristan, and immediately, hurt is painted on his face.

Fuck.

"Hey, Levi," Tristan shouts back. "We're over in"—he scans the shelves behind me—"Nordic Noir." His expression softens as he face palms and adds, "We were looking for a cookbook and got lost. Looking for a good Swedish meatball recipe."

Tristan and I can hardly contain our laughter when a man rounds the corner and looks between us. "Pretty sure there are enough meatballs in my store. Please don't add any more."

"Oh, come on. That's cheesy as fuck, even for you, eh?" Tristan replies, as if nothing happened between us.

"I should go," I offer and move past both of them.

Tristan catches me by the wrist. "I'll see you later?" I nod, and it's enough for him to release me.

After stopping at the florist, I get a ride home from a man who must be the only ride-share driver in town, based on how long it took for him to pick me up. I'll have to put off the trip to the hardware store for another day. I had to get away from Tristan, away from the pleasantries of the people in Coal's.

I retreat to my parent's spare bedroom, suddenly wishing I had stayed at the lodge. I hate that Jamie's Lodge is always sold out for tourist season. If I had planned ahead, I could've blocked off a room, but a late booking in December would mean I'd be hopping from room to room for a month.

I shrug out of my coat that I should throw away at this point; I highly doubt the local dry cleaner could get eggnog out of it. I then strip out of the rest of my clothes and hop in the shower.

Turning on the faucet extra hot, I let the water warm. After a minute, I step in, relishing the sting of the heat in contrast to the cool winter air that manages to seep into the house. No matter how hard I try, my thoughts drift back to Tristan in the bookstore.

His mischievous smile.

The way he let me take control.

How I'd give anything to have one night with him.

I fist my cock, wishing it was his hand and not mine. Bracing myself on the shower wall, I let myself give in to the fantasy...

Falling to my knees for him.

Teasing his cock with my tongue until he begs for more.

The feel of his cum down my throat.

Turning him around, ripping down his jeans, and fucking that perfect ass of his until he's screaming my name...

"Tristan," I groan as I come harder than I have in a long fucking time. My cum paints the shower wall, and it takes a solid minute for me to catch my breath.

I detach the showerhead from its mount to spray away the evidence. Replacing the head, I let the hot water beat down on me, taking a moment to get him off my mind. I shouldn't be thinking of him like this. We aren't even friends anymore and there's no way he feels the same way about me.

He did kiss me, though...

Fuck, maybe I have this all wrong.

Once I'm cleaned up, I exit the shower, goosebumps erupting down my arms from the cold air. At least that's what I'm telling myself. I'm half-tempted to live in the hot shower for the foreseeable future.

How the fuck am I going to survive a month here, when after one day, I'm jerking off in the shower, thinking about him?

TRISTAN

D*amn it.*
Fuck.

Shit. Fuck. Damn it.

Why did I kiss him?

I've been pacing my old bedroom at my parents' place, wondering what the fuck I'm going to do about Myles. I haven't seen him for years, and in less than a day, I'm practically dry humping him in my friend's bookstore.

I glance out the window to the house next door. *Why is he back? Why now?* I rake my hands roughly through my hair and sit on the edge of the bed. How am I going to avoid him for a whole month, especially with the holidays coming up?

A soft knock at the door pulls me out of my downward spiral.

"Yeah?"

My sister, Beth, enters cautiously. She leans against the door frame, inspecting her nails. "I'm sure you heard."

Beth's in her usual flannel and jeans but has more makeup on than she typically wears. She's definitely wanting to impress someone. Probably Axl at Jamie's Lodge, even though she always denies it when I ask.

Resting my elbows on my knees, I sigh, "And saw."

"And? Is he as hot as you remember?" Beth teases.

Hotter.

"I kissed him," I admit. Her eyes widen and she sucks in a breath. "Yeah, I know." I can't help the smirk tugging at my lips. "But he kissed me back."

Beth gasps. "Tris!" There's an unmistakable twinkle in her eyes. She's been wanting me to reach out to Myles for years, but I always change the subject when she brings him up.

"I know, I shouldn't have done it, but it felt right."

"Well, maybe he came by for seconds?"

I frown and ask, "What?"

"He's downstairs... *for you*." Beth wiggles her eyebrows suggestively.

"Don't fuck with me."

"Go see for yourself." She leaves my room as if she didn't just tell me the one man I've always wanted, but never wanted me, is downstairs.

But he kissed me back.

"Beth," I call after her but she doesn't turn. "*Shit,*" I mutter aloud.

"He'll be right down," she tells him loud enough that I can hear, then adds, "I'm headed out. See you later!" Her voice sings, with an echo upstairs.

I wipe my sweaty hands on my jeans. I offered to take care of his dry cleaning, maybe that's why he's here…

Yes. That's it. Dry cleaning.

I head downstairs, nervous as fuck. When I reach the last step, he looks up from his phone and stuffs it in his pocket.

Did he get hotter in the last hour? How the hell is that possible?

"Hey," I say, unsure how the hell to greet him after having my tongue down his throat.

"You kissed me." His expression is unreadable, his voice devoid of all emotion.

"Sorry, 'bout that. I didn't mean—"

Myles closes the distance, making me lose my train of thought. He grips my shirt and brings our faces mere inches apart. "Do it again."

"I—"

"Do it again," he repeats. "This time, without your friend walking in."

Our mouths collide in a fevered kiss that's beyond toe-curling—it's cock-twitching. His tongue duals with mine and I'm unsure if either of us have the upperhand here. I simultaneously want to take charge and surrender to him. Either way, I pull him closer.

Myles reaches his hand between us, palming my cock through my pants. As much as I want this, I reluctantly pull back. I don't want some casual hook up, especially with him. He's only here for a month, and seeing him today has already unearthed feelings I buried years ago.

"I'm sorry, I can't do this," I admit.

"Fuck." He rakes a hand through his hair. "You have a boyfriend or a—" He pauses, swallowing hard before asking, "Are you married?"

He glances at my ringless hand. I lift it, wiggling my fingers, confirming I am indeed single. "No, it's not that." I stuff my hands in my pockets and take a deep breath. "I should go. I, uh, need to head back into town. I told Samuel I'd help him on his package delivery route today. Something about needing help with all the wine orders and obnoxiously large boxes after the Black Friday sales." I'm not supposed to help him until tomorrow, but I can't be in the same room with Myles right now.

"What are you doing tonight?"

"There's the tree lighting. I have to help Helly and Neil prep for it; the cafe is always busy when there's town events."

He chuckles. "Is there anyone you don't help in town?"

"Not really." I shrug. "When I returned after my injury, everyone took care of me. The least I can do is return the favor." Myles nods with a furrowed brow, as if he's carefully considering something. When he doesn't say anything, I offer, "I know you hate Christmas, but do you want to come help tonight?"

"I don't hate Christmas," he scoffs. I raise an eyebrow, and he corrects, "I just don't *like* it."

"Still a bit of a Scrooge, eh? Seems some things never change." I shake my head and chuckle. "I'll walk you out."

Myles was always the quiet one; he kept to himself throughout most of our childhood. The man before me is someone else entirely. His jaw tics and I'm pretty sure he's not used to being told no.

He reluctantly follows me to the front door. As he reaches for the handle, I stop him, covering his hand with mine. The question that's been weighing on me tumbles from my lips, "Why haven't you been back to Coal's before now?"

Staring at our joined hands, he sighs and admits, "I was in love with someone who only saw me as a friend. I couldn't bear the thought of coming home for the holidays and finding out he was married with two kids and a goldendoodle."

"You were in..." *No. There's no fucking way.*

Myles lifts his gaze to me. "Yeah. I didn't know how to tell you. I moved to another fucking country to avoid it."

I slide his hand away from the door, interlacing our fingers. "I would be married with two kids and a goldendoodle, but the man I wanted to do it with moved to another country."

He squeezes my hand. "Don't fuck with me, Tris."

"I'm not. But I'll admit, I always wanted to."

His eyes dart between mine as we both try to make sense of this. For years, I thought my feelings were one-sided. Apparently, he thought the same. I know it's going to hurt when he leaves at the end of the month, but it'll hurt more if I spend the next month wondering what it would be like to be with him.

In an instant, he grips the back of my neck and his mouth crashes into mine. It's messy and frenzied, neither one of us can get close enough. He kicks off his shoes and backs me up until I'm pressed against the cold wood door. I tear off his jacket, and as I'm reaching for his belt, he swats my hand away and growls between kisses, "You can have this cock after you've come down my throat."

"Then get on your fucking knees." My commanding tone surprises even me. He chuckles against my lips. A bit embarrassed, I add, "Sorry, I mean, if you want to."

Myles laughs harder. "Fuck, I lo—" He stills and breaks our kiss, pulling back an inch and caging me in with his hands on either side of me. His wide eyes search mine.

My breath uneven and ragged, I manage, "Say it." *Please*.

He steps back and unbuttons his shirt, shrugging it off and tossing it on top of his coat. Taking a fistful of his shirt from the nape of his neck, he pulls it up and over his head, then adds it to the pile of discarded clothes. He closes the distance and wets his lips, my gaze falling to them.

"Make me," he purrs.

I swipe my thumb across his bottom lip, then grip his chin to bring him less than an inch away, our lips nearly touching. "Hard to hear what you're saying while I'm fucking your face."

He smirks and falls to his knees, avoiding saying the one thing I've wanted to hear all these years. In one swift motion, he drags my pants and boxer briefs down to my knees. He licks the underside of my cock, swirls his tongue around the tip, then takes me in his mouth until I'm hitting the back of his throat.

"Fuck," I moan, gripping his hair. He doesn't move, instead massaging my cock with his tongue and relaxing his throat until he's taken all of me. He sucks hard as he pulls off me and replaces his mouth with his hand. After feeling his warm, wet mouth, he tortures me by stroking up and down my length before my cock finally slides across his tongue again. I instinctively thrust deeper. His light gag spurs me on, and I guide him until he's taken all of me again.

Myles grips my ass; his fingers dig into me for leverage as I fuck his mouth with short, controlled thrusts. The vibration from his moans nearly make me come. I groan, holding back my imminent orgasm for as long as possible. I've waited too long for this moment; I can't finish this early. He slides a hand down my leg and unzips his pants, freeing his cock.

Is that a... fuck. He has a ladder.

He strokes himself and the thought of his pierced cock fucking me, coupled with watching him, is enough to have me spilling down his throat as I moan his name. *So much for not finishing early...*

As I begin to pull him off me, he looks up with dark eyes, swallowing every last drop as he holds me in place. He continues massaging my cock with his tongue, not taking his eyes off me.

I can't catch my breath. He keeps my hard cock in his mouth as he continues his slow strokes. My cock twitches and he chuckles, finally pulling away.

Myles stands and I can't help reaching for his cock, loving the contrast of his piercings against his smooth skin. He groans, "I hope you have lube upstairs. We're going to need it. A fuck-ton of it."

MYLES

I just sucked off the man I've craved for most of my life. This can't be real. Today is a dream. It's the only explanation. I'm going to wake up from it any minute now and find that none of this happened.

I slipped and almost told him I love him. If we were together I'd fall for him again, but I didn't want the first time those words to pass my lips to be like this. As much as I've wanted him, I don't know if he's looking for a casual fuck or if he was serious when he said he imagined being with me. What would that even look like for us?

I'm lost in thought when Tristan kisses me deeply, carefully stroking me. I have a feeling he's never been with someone who's pierced; he's cautious and avoiding too tight of a grip. I cover his hand with mine, guiding him to use a pressure I'm comfortable with.

"I have a confession to make," he whispers against my lips. "I've only ever been a top, I've never…"

"Been fucked?"

"Yeah," he chuckles and pulls back. "I mean, I've had toys up my ass before."

I'd be his first?

"Well, I don't think fucking you at your front door is the best idea," I tease.

"True." He tries to smother a smile but his dimples appear anyway.

Tristan takes my hand, I can't help laughing to myself at both of our cocks still hanging out. He tugs up his pants with his free hand. I tuck myself back into my boxer briefs; no need to make this any more weird than it already is.

He guides us past the living room and upstairs. It gives me flashbacks of when we were younger, when I hoped for a day like this—where we were more than just friends.

Family portraits still line the walls leading upstairs. I pause, seeing one of both of our families from when we were in high school. Tristan looks back at me with a small smile. "Oh, yeah, Mom and Pop love that one." He huffs a laugh. "I think your parents have the same one in their house."

My parents always knew I liked Tristan and regularly told me to tell him. If I had worked up the nerve, maybe I would've never left Coal's. I've built an empire since I left. What would've happened if I stayed?

We continue up the stairs and into his old bedroom. It's a blast from the past with hockey trophies and the same wallpaper from the early 90s; the only difference is the dark navy comforter.

"Have you been staying here since you moved back?"

He looks around for a moment and laughs. "Fuck no. I have a small apartment in town. I was just helping Pop with a few things around the house before heading out tonight. He just ran to the hardware store to pick up bulb replacements for the Christmas lights."

There's an awkward silence between us. Until now, things today have felt easy. Maybe being back in this room has resurfaced the nervousness I felt as a teen.

"This is weird, right?" he asks nervously.

"Weird as fuck," I confirm with a small laugh. "We don't have to do—"

Tristan shuts me up as his lips crush mine.

"Shut up, Myles," he growls as he nips at my bottom lip. "I know you probably just want a quick fuck, but I'll fucking take it."

"Whoa." I press my hands against his chest, giving myself an inch to clarify, "I never said I wanted a quick fuck. For one, it sure as hell wouldn't be quick." I can't bring myself to tell him I don't do casual; I'm scared he doesn't want the same thing as me. Instead, I just kiss him.

Since he's never had anyone fuck him before, and I enjoy both fucking and being fucked, I'll take him any way he wants me to. I drop my pants and my cock jets out. I sweep a few beads of precum off the tip, swirling it around the head. Considering I jerked off in the shower earlier, I'm probably going to last longer than he could handle for our first time.

"Sit down," I command. Tristan sits on his bed, and without me asking, he takes my cock in his hand and swirls his tongue around the tip. He slowly takes me in his mouth, my piercings gliding along his tongue one at a time. "Do you want me to come in your mouth or your ass?"

He chokes at the question and pulls off me. "I, um, I guess, uh…"

Fuck, he's adorable. I stroke my cock a few times, then sit on the bed with him. "I like to give and receive, is that ok?"

Tristan chuckles. "Pretty sure we'll need a five-gallon tub of lube to get through the month." He surprises me by knocking me back onto the bed. He stands, leaning over me and bracing his hands on either side of my head. "I don't know what I'm doing, but I want that bedazzled cock of yours."

He pushes from the bed and rummages through his nightstand, pulling out a bottle of lube. Squeezing a fair amount into his hands, he slathers my cock with it before capping it up and putting it away. I still have that feeling, like no time has passed. His touch is familiar, even though he's never had my cock in his hand or mouth before today.

"Alright, let's do this," he playfully commands. I have to keep myself from laughing at the way he's psyching himself up for this.

I feel like a damn virgin with him, fumbling through this. Since I'm only a few inches taller than him, standing might work best. I get up and guide him to the wall, placing his hands against it. His breathing picks up.

"If anything is too much, you have to tell me," I insist, kissing his neck. He nods.

I pull his shirt over his head and toss it onto the bed, trailing kisses down his back as I fall to my knees. Taking the waistband of his boxer briefs between my teeth, I pull them over his ass and drag them down his legs. I nip at one of his ass cheeks before spreading them, licking from his balls up his crack. His ass puckers, and I resist laughing at how sensitive he is to my touch. I fucking love it.

I lick around his asshole, then wet my finger and slowly press in two knuckles deep. His breath hitches and he lets out a groan. I take my time stretching him out, then pull it out and swipe some lube from my cock before adding a second finger.

"Fuck, that feels good," he hisses. I lick and suck on his balls as I drive my fingers deeper. He relaxes, unclenching from my fingers. If he keeps breathing, he can take me.

I keep my fingers inside him as I stand, kissing up his back to his shoulder. "I'll go slow this time, but I can't guarantee I'll be so gentle next time." I withdraw my fingers and rub the length of my cock up and down his ass, then push in—just the tip. I bite down on his shoulder, stifling a groan. He feels too fucking good.

Slowly entering him inch by inch, I feel a slight tug on each piercing as it enters him, until he takes all of me. He arches his back and pushes back into me, my piercings rubbing inside him as I fuck him deeper.

"Fuck, Tris, you take me so well. You were fucking made for this," I whisper, nipping at his ear.

I slowly thrust in and out of him as he adjusts to me. I've imagined fucking him no less than a thousand times, but I never imagined it would feel this good. He meets my thrusts, keeping one hand braced on the wall and the other stroking his cock. I pick up my pace as he chases his orgasm; he's close, based on how he's tightening around me. I grip his hips tightly and drive into him harder, but not faster.

"I'm close," he pants.

"You don't come until I say you come," I grit out.

"Fuck, why is that so hot?" he laughs.

I can't help but chuckle. I thrust inside him and hold, reaching around to grab his cock. I keep the same pace he did; he can't hold on much longer. I sink my teeth into his shoulder, then whisper, "Come with me."

He groans and comes in my hand, his ass clenching around my cock as he moans my name. For years, I fantasized about hearing him come. I still can't believe I'm buried deep inside him with his cock in my hand. It's enough to make me come harder than I have in my life.

"Fuck, you're amazing," I mutter, kissing his shoulder as my cock twitches inside him.

After today, there's no way in hell I could ever be with another man. He's fucking ruined me.

There's a soft knock on his bedroom door, followed by his mom asking, "Tris? If you're done with your friend in there, maybe invite him to dinner. We need to eat early with the tree lighting later."

Tristan sucks in a breath and replies, "Uh, sure, we'll be right down," then whispers to me, "I'm so sorry."

He winces as I slowly pull out of him. I don't wait to hear retreating footsteps, I turn him around and fucking devour his mouth, unable to get enough of him. I chuckle against his lips, "Well, are you going to invite me to dinner, or what?"

TRISTAN

M yles looks down at his bare chest, then back at me. "I left my clothes downstairs."

"Shit." I push past him to my old closet to see what I have that might fit him. I sift through dozens of old shirts, settling on a couple that aren't too worn and two pairs of gray sweatpants. I return to him and hand him the clothes. "Sorry, that's all I have here." He tosses the pile on the bed, slips off his slacks, then puts on a shirt and sweatpants. "You, um, you can keep those." I make quick work to get dressed. Things are awkward enough as is, no need to add to it with my dick hanging out.

Tying the string on the sweatpants, Myles glances up at me through his lashes. "Oh, I intend to." He pauses for a second, then his eyes widen. "Fuck, one second." He gets up and walks to my ensuite bathroom. The water runs for a minute before he returns with a wet washcloth. "Turn around."

I do as he asks and he tugs down my sweatpants, carefully cleaning between my asscheeks with the warm cloth. I wince; my ass is sore but I relish the ache. When he's finished, he kisses my shoulder, and pulls up my sweats.

"Do you want to stay for dinner?" I ask hopefully.

"I would but I should probably check in with my Pop. I forgot the tree lighting was tonight until you mentioned it, so I'm sure he has something over-the-top planned. You know how much he loves Christmas." He shrugs and stuffs his hands in his pockets. It pulls the fabric taut, making the outline of his cock more prevalent.

Stop staring, weirdo.

"Your family loves the holidays, why do you hate it so much?"

"Oh, um, it doesn't matter." His jaw tics and he adds, "I should probably get going."

That's it? He's just going to fuck me and leave? I'm such a fucking idiot.

"Yeah, ok. I, uh, need to get downstairs." I'm not sure what else to say. The energy between us, that was electric minutes ago, is now making my stomach turn.

I need to get far, far away from Myles Fucking Comet.

Without another word, I leave my old room. Thankfully, he follows. We make our way downstairs and I'm met with the distinct smell of my mother's favourite store bought pumpkin loaf that she puts in the oven to pretend she made it from scratch.

She pulls it out of the oven with expert timing. "Oh! Hi, boys. Myles, I heard you were back for Christmas; it's so good to see you."

Mom sets the loaf on a cooling rack; she's nothing if not committed. She rounds the kitchen island to greet Myles, bringing him in for a tight hug. "We missed you," she sighs, not letting him out of her embrace.

He chuckles softly. "Missed you too, Mrs. Anderson."

She snorts. "Don't make me sound like some old tart. You're a grown ass man now. Please, call me Liv."

Finally releasing Myles, she wanders back into the kitchen to slice up the bread. "You're staying for dinner." It's not a question; it never is with my mother.

This is already so messed up, I need him gone. Thankfully, he declines, "I am actually headed next door. My pop—" he begins.

"Is coming over with your mom," she finishes. *Fuck my life.* "I invited them over a few hours ago." *Of course you did.* "I figured we could all have a quick dinner and head to the tree lighting early, since Tris is helping Helly and Neil and I'm selling mistletoe bundles to fundraise for the tree lighting. We were short this year, so every little bit helps."

"Oh. Um, ok. I'll run next door and change."

Busying herself looking for something in the pantry, she tells him, "Wonderful, we'll see you in an hour. Oh, and don't forget, your clothes are still by the front door."

Fuuuuuuck.

Dinner was—thankfully—uneventful, mostly filled with questions around what Myles has been up to since he left. His parents shared their plans for the next month; they love the holidays and always have. Even Myles did, until the Christmas after we both came out to our families.

That year, I wanted to ask him to the Christmas formal, but I lost my nerve. Because no one at school knew I was gay, I took Pepper Iverton to the dance. I was the hockey prodigy, and she was the beautiful, blonde cheerleader everyone wanted. It seemed like a great way to mask everything.

That Christmas, everything changed. Myles stopped talking to me, professional hockey teams started looking at me, and life became a bit of a blur. To this day, I couldn't tell you what happened during the last few years of high school—it was a fucking shit show.

Everything is set for the tree lighting. Mr. Comet helped Helly, Neil, and I set everything up. Mrs. Comet assisted with decorations, while my parents finished setting up the fundraiser booth. A last minute anonymous donation came in to cover the costs, and I'm pretty sure it was Myles, but he's nowhere to be found.

All of Coal's Lake comes out for the lighting. I've only been back for a couple of years, but it's exactly as I remember. Except, when I was younger, I thought I would be coming back home in the middle of hockey season with a husband, our kids, and even a damn goldendoodle. Instead, I'm single as fuck, just had my high school crush avoid me after his pierced cock was inside me, and my hockey career is over.

Since Helly and Neil seem to have everything under control, I slink out of the event and go home. My ass still hurts and I want to curl up under a thick, weighted blanket and forget today ever happened.

Hopefully, Myles will leave early and I'll be able to enjoy the holidays in peace.

MYLES

Tristan has been avoiding me for a week. I've come up with no less than five unique reasons to stop by his parent's house, and I've run out of ideas. I can't bring myself to ask his parents, or mine, where he lives, so I get dressed in a shawl-collared sweater and jeans, take extra time to groom my beard, and ensure the rest of my appearance is flawless. My hope is to run into him while grabbing an almond milk latte at The Reindeer Cafe.

Early evening coffee is normal, right?

I grab my freshly dry-cleaned coat and the keys to my pop's truck when the doorbell rings. Hoping it's Tristan, I set the jacket by the door and take a deep breath before answering it. My face falls when I see it's just a parcel delivery man.

"Evening, sir. I've got a package here for Myles Comet."

"That's me," I confirm, but no one knows I'm here. Who the hell would send me a package?

"I'm required to let you know that your package is damaged and ask if you'd still like to accept it."

I glance down at the box that looks like it's been to hell and back. Inside, *Water-Based Lube* is scrawled in bright red letters on the top of a bucket.

What the actual fuck?

"You must have the wrong house." It's not the wrong house. The words Tristan said to me about a bucket of lube are ringing in my ears. My jaw tics and my fists ball at my sides. He won't talk to me but he'll send me fucking lube?

"It doesn't seem that the actual product was damaged, sir, but you do have the right to deny deliv—"

"No," I insist, reaching into my pocket, pulling out my wallet. "I'll give you a thousand dollars to never tell a fucking soul about this."

"Oh, I can't accept tips, Mr. Comet."

"It's not a tip." I shove the money into his coat pocket. I leave him on the front porch to discard the obscenely large tub of lube in the trash on the side of the house.

I'm done with this shit; we're not in high school anymore. Once the delivery driver leaves, I text my mom for Tristan's number. She replies with his number, and I quickly type out a message to him along with a picture of the bucket in the trash.

> Thanks for the lube.

I almost add "asshole" but think better of it. There is still a slim possibility he didn't send it.

TRISTAN
Who is this?

I roll my eyes; I can't tell if he's being serious or not. I click the video call button. His face lights up the screen, and before he gets a word out, my own tumble from me, "Why are you avoiding me?"

"Avoiding you? What are you talking about?" He appears honestly confused.

"I went to the tree lighting, and you left and haven't been by your parents' place in a week."

His expression softens and he laughs, "Not all of us are millionaires. Some of us have to work, you know. I only played a few years pro, it all dried up. In case you forgot, I teach five days a week. The kids are getting ready for the Christmas formal and it's finals. It's busy as fuck."

I still the moment I hear 'Christmas formal.' The whole fucking reason I can't even look at a damn Christmas tree without my heart breaking is the Christmas formal after we both came out. He took Pepper, even though I sent him a candy gram asking him to go with me. They spent the evening cozied up to each other and it solidified that he never saw me as more than a friend.

I swallow hard, stuffing down my hurt from years ago and change the subject. "Fine, so you're not avoiding me. Why was a bucket of lube delivered to my parent's house for me?"

"Fuck if I know, I—" His eyes widen. "One second." The screen turns black but I can still hear him. There's a gasp, a laugh and an "oh shit."

"Tris?"

The video comes back into view. "Ok, so the night of the tree ceremony, I, um... I sort of had one too many to drink."

"And, what? Ordered a drum of lube?"

"It appears so," he winces.

I can't help but laugh. "Really, Tris?"

"I don't know! I was drunk and probably thought it was funny. I don't remember doing it, but it totally sounds like me. I'm sorry, I— wait, did you say you were at the tree lighting?"

"Yeah, I was late because the truck had a flat. Had to call a tow truck to help me out—Kris Kringle Towing." I chuckle. "Fitting."

He frowns. "But you hate Christmas."

"I hate Christmas because of you," I blurt.

"Me? What do you mean you hate Christmas because of me?"

I shake my head. "It doesn't matter."

"Oh, no. We aren't doing this. You're not going to drop some kind of ominous statement like that, and then disappear for years again. Why is it my fault you hate Christmas?"

I shut my eyes tight and reluctantly admit, "Pepper Iverton."

"What the fuck does... Wait a fucking minute. You mean to tell me that you hate Christmas because I took a fucking beard to a school dance?"

"Beard or not, you took her instead of me," I snap.

Fuck, this escalated quickly.

"It was years ago!" he counters. "It's not like you would've said yes if I asked you."

"I asked *you!*" I yell.

"What the fuck are you talking about? You never asked me."

I blow out a deep breath and do my best to keep my emotions in check, even though all I want to do is scream. "It was years ago, just forget I said anything."

"No," he growls. "Fucking say what you were going to say. I lost my best friend—who I was in love with—over some sort of miscommunication, so I want to hear what you think happened."

I begin pacing up and down my parents' porch. "I bought a candy gram to ask you to the dance. You never replied, and you took her instead. I went stag, and the whole night you were sitting and laughing with her. It hurt, Tris. When we came out at the same time, I thought..." The words catch in my throat, unable to escape.

Tristan shakes his head. "I loved you. Don't you get that? I never got a fucking candy gram. If I had, I would've said yes and it would've made my whole fucking year. I didn't have plans to out myself to everyone, but I would've, for you. Pepper? She was obsessed with my buddy Mason; I was giving her pointers for flirting with him. They're married now, by the way. *Fuck!*" He groans. "Is that why you left? Is that why you hate Christmas and never came back home?"

Yes. "No. It didn't help, though." I can't bring myself to admit it.

"What do you want, Myles?"

"What do *you* want?" I counter.

"Fine, don't answer me. It doesn't matter what I want, anyway. You're leaving in a few weeks and who the fuck knows when I'll see you again. I'm not going to get my hopes up that you're going to have some big grand gesture where you stay here in Coal's like a damn book or movie. This is real life. I want someone who won't just tell me he wants the happily ever after, but works for it. You and I could've been together this whole fucking time if our pride hadn't gotten in the way. I'm done with that shit."

I shake my head and laugh to myself. "We're fucking idiots."

"Yep, and you have a bucket of lube to prove it. Look, I'm sorry I didn't tell you how I felt years ago. I know trying to start something a couple weeks before Christmas is fucking stupid—"

"Text me your address, right now." He's about to protest, so I add, "I'll get it from someone else if you don't."

I hang up the video call. A moment later Tristan texts me the address to his apartment. I don't know if I'll stay in Coal's Lake after Christmas. I don't know if Tristan will want to be with me, even if I did. But I know, with all of my being, that if I don't at least try to fix this, I'll regret it for the rest of my life.

TRISTAN

Myles Comet is my kryptonite. I shouldn't have him in my apartment. All it'll take is that little smirk he gets, biting his lip, and I'm fucking toast.

Fifteen minutes after we hung up, there's a knock at the door. My hand poised on the handle, I blow out a long breath before opening it. "Hey." It's the only word I can manage. He's wearing an oatmeal, shawl-collared sweater and dark denim—looking like he stepped out of a damn magazine ad.

Damn. Why is he so hot?

No. Fuck. Stop it.

I must be staring too long because his fucking smirk appears as he asks, "Can I come in?"

Swinging the door wider, I clear my throat. "Right, sorry 'bout that."

This is a terrible idea.

Thankfully, he didn't spot the mistletoe above my door. I don't need a cute romantic gesture right now. I'm not sure why my mother insisted on putting it up. "*You never know when it might come in handy,*" she teased, adding in something about having a "gentleman caller." I know she wants me to settle down and start a family, but I want to marry someone who's my best friend, who makes me a better man. That's hard to find in a small town of only ten thousand people, where only a handful of them are gay or bi.

"Would you like a cup of tea, or…?" I offer.

Myles walks further into my apartment and takes a seat on the couch, hunched over and resting his elbows on his knees. He wrings his hands and replies, "No, I'm fine. I just need to get this off my chest, if that's ok?"

I'm torn between sitting next to him and keeping as much space between us as possible. I opt for distance and start a kettle on the stove. While waiting for the water to heat, I lean against the counter, arms folded over my chest. "Alright, out with it then."

"You were my best friend. When we came out, I secretly hoped you were into me. I was afraid of saying anything because I thought you only saw me as a friend. I didn't want to lose you. We normally spent Christmases together but after you rejected me…" He shakes his head. "I know you said you didn't see it, but I was young and it fucking hurt. I used to love Christmas. I haven't ever since."

"So, what now? You're gone in a couple weeks. You think we can have some kind of small town romance, where the rich guy finds the meaning of Christmas and we live happily ever after? I know your mom loves those movies"—*so do I, but I'm sure as fuck not admitting it*—"but logistically, it's not realistic."

"Why the fuck not? If I moved here, would you consider giving us a shot?"

Yes. "I don't know. It's all hypothetical."

Myles stands and prowls toward me, his eyes dark. I stay rooted in place and remind myself to keep my clothes on, even if my cock twitches in my pants at the thought of ripping them off right here in my kitchen. Once we are toe-to-toe, he stops. His heated gaze softens as he pleads, "Let's make it not hypothetical."

"You still hate Christmas. It would never work," I tease.

"Give me until New Years."

"Our parents have four hundred things on our calendars between now and then. When would we see each other?"

"We'll go to everything together." He takes my hand and places it over his heart. "Be mine until New Years. We can figure out the rest when—"

"When you leave. This is a shitty idea, Myles."

"Do you have a better one?"

Move in with me and don't leave Coal's. "Not really. But if this is going to work, you can't hate Christmas anymore."

"Then, make me not hate Christmas." He wets his lips, and it takes everything in me to not take those soft lips between my teeth.

"Fine." I playfully pinch his sweater. "This won't do."

I step away from him and head to my bedroom to find the ugliest fucking sweater I can find. I have no less than eight that I've collected over the years. While rummaging through my drawers, I call over my shoulder, "Take off your shirt." I hear the rustling of fabric and look behind me, finding him stripping off his sweater and tee and tossing them onto my bed. "Oh, sorry, I thought you were still in the kitchen." I can't tear my eyes away from his bare chest. Myles has an athletic build with lean muscles; he obviously works out but doesn't bulk up. It's a stark contrast from years ago when he didn't have an ounce of muscle on him.

I playfully toss an obnoxious ugly Christmas sweater at him, complete with sewn on jingle bells, and take off my shirt. He doesn't put his on, and when my arms are in the sleeves of mine, ready to put over my head, he rips the sweater off me. It falls to the ground and, in an instant, his lips are on mine. His fingers tangle in my hair as he deepens our kiss, his tongue exploring as if he's trying to memorize every inch of my mouth. I grip his back and pull him impossibly closer.

Myles hands slide down my body, reaching for the button of my pants. "We can do the cheesy made-for-TV Christmas stuff later. Right now, I want you to fuck me so hard I'm not able to sit for a week," he murmurs against my lips.

"Should've brought your bucket of lube," I chuckle.

I fumble, trying to unbutton his pants. Once they're unfastened, he makes quick work to kick off his shoes and take off his pants and boxer briefs. "On the bed," I growl.

He sits as I take off my pants. His gaze rakes my body, landing on my hard cock. I stroke myself slowly, his eyes darken as he watches me. Climbing onto the bed, he scoots back and I nudge his legs apart as he lays back on the bed, bracing myself with a hand on either side of his head. He cups his hand behind my neck and pulls me in to kiss him. This kiss is different from his other kisses; it's not sexy or playful, it's raw and emotional. He's pouring years of missed touches and kisses into one heated moment. My heart squeezes at the idea that this could be more than just a Christmas fling—this could be real.

I break our kiss to grab the lube from my nightstand. I squeeze a fair amount into my hand and stroke my cock to make sure I get enough on the tip and down my shaft. With a little left on my hand, I swipe my fingers up and down his ass. He grips the back of my neck and hisses, "Fuck, I need you, Tris."

I lean in to kiss him briefly, and as I grind my length against him twice, his grip tightens. I line up my cock and, inch by inch, push inside him. I sit back, my gaze falling to his ass, swallowing my cock beautifully. I can't help my long, slow thrusts, wanting to savor each one. I love watching him take all of me.

Myles pulls his knees up and I spread his legs wider, getting even deeper than before. His perfect, heavily pierced cock slaps against his stomach with each thrust. "Harder," he groans and grips his cock, matching my rhythm as I roughly fuck him.

His ass is tight, and I don't know how much longer I'll last. The claps of his ass against my thighs and the wet sounds of fucking him fill the room. My breath uneven, I grit out, "I'm close, but don't you dare come. I'm taking it all. I want to taste you on my tongue the rest of the night."

I thrust harder, and as I come, I bend down to kiss him. I slowly pump in and out of him as I empty myself inside him. My whole body is vibrating and my vision blurs as he pulls me closer, deepening our kiss. I'm sex-drunk but I know it's more than that. I'd give anything for this to last more than a few weeks.

I slowly pull out of him and trail kisses along his jaw, down his neck, and nip and suck until a light bruise appears. For now, he's mine, and I want the whole fucking world to know it. I move down his body until I reach his stomach and take his cock in my hand, stroking twice before sliding it into my mouth. The contrast of the cool metal and his warm cock on my tongue is unlike anything I've experienced before. I take all of him, flicking each piercing with my tongue.

"Shit, Tris, that feels so fucking good." The praise spurs me on and I continue teasing the fuck out of him. "I can't take it," he pants. There's an audible pop as I pull my mouth off him.

I take his hands and guide them to the back of my head. "Show me how you want it. Fuck my face until there's tears painting my cheeks." He grips my hair and thrusts up, fucking my mouth.

"Fuck, it's too much. Relax your throat." I do and choke a little, my eyes watering as I take him deeper. "*Fuck.* Just like that. Shit, I'm going to—"

With a final thrust, he comes for me, moaning my name. He's so deep, all I feel is his cock twitching against my tongue as his cum spills down my throat in small bursts.

I swallow and slowly lick each barbell clean as I pull off him.

"Tris, that was..."

"Yeah," I chuckle.

"Fuck it, I'm not asking, I'm staying over."

I'm not sure what this is between us, so I make light of it, "You just want to wake up to me slowly fucking you, with my hand wrapped around your cock."

Myles sits up and captures my mouth with his in a searing kiss I feel all the way to my toes. "No... I mean, sure, but that's not why I want to stay over."

I chuckle against his lips, "You'd rather me wake you up with your cock in my mouth?"

He pinches my side. "Smartass. I have to make up for lost years with you. But, we're never going to leave your apartment, are we?"

"Are you kidding me? I'm going to fuck you in no less than a hundred different places in town before New Year's."

He laughs and glances at the discarded Christmas sweaters. "Guess we better get started, then."

TRISTAN

CHRISTMAS EVE

The Comets normally spend Christmas Eve with mine, but Myles' dad was a bit overzealous with the decorations this year and their power has been out for two days. They've been staying here the last two nights. With one of the biggest storms of the year today, Myles and I need to stay as well. Laying in my too-small bed, watching a corny as fuck Christmas movie, Myles and I are about to live the cliché one-bed trope tonight... he just doesn't know it yet.

My mom texted me half an hour ago but I haven't told Myles because, as I've found these past few weeks, he's a fucking grump when things don't go as planned.

As soon as the movie is over, he asks, "What time do you want to head to your place?"

"Let me check the roads." I scroll the weather app on my phone. After successfully avoiding telling him, I'm hoping I can sell my disappointment, despite not caring whether we stay here or not tonight. "Oh no! It looks like the storm is too bad to drive in. We'll have to stay here for the night."

Nailed it.

"We're snowed in?" Myles asks with fear in his eyes. "We were just snowed in a few days ago!" At least last time, we were at my apartment. I knew he wouldn't be thrilled about staying here with both of our families.

"I know you have cabin fever, but there's nothing we can do about it. It's not my fault your dad needed more lights on the house and you lost power," I grumble.

He sighs. "I was really hoping we could spend Christmas together, just the two of us."

"Maybe next year," I playfully say with a wink.

I shouldn't joke about it. We have one week left. One week before he's supposed to go back home. The last two weeks were spent creating new Christmas memories to make up for the ones we lost, and the one that could've been saved if we weren't idiots when we were kids. *And also fucking all over town.*

We can't make the same mistake twice; I can't go years wondering "what if."

Myles didn't think my little joke was funny either. His sad eyes pierce me like a knife to the heart. I blow out a long breath and muster up the courage to ask the one thing I hadn't dared to ask these past few weeks. "Move back to Coal's."

Ok, so maybe not a question. I don't want to ask, anyway. I want him here.

He doesn't have a chance to respond; there's a knock at the door. "Hey guys, mom said she has something for all of us. I swear to Loki if there's matching Christmas pyjamas..." Beth's voice trails off as she moves away from the door.

I secretly hope there are matching pyjamas, knowing Myles will be about as thrilled about it as my sister. I smile at the thought, but it quickly evaporates the moment I'm brought back to the realization that his business, his life... none of it is here. He has no reason to stay.

As much as I try to keep things light with a painted-on grin, I'm sure my disappointment is still in my tone when I ask, "Should we head downstairs?"

All I really want to do is ask him to stay. I don't. I move to get up but he grips my wrist.

"Yes," he replies with a light huff and a small smile that meets his eyes. "Yes, I'll move back to Coal's Lake."

I suck in a breath. *Did I hear him right?*

His eyes twinkling, he continues, "Tris, I have enough money that I could sell my company and never work another day in my life. I've only been here a few weeks, and while I think we could stand to get a bigger place, I want to move back. Maybe get a goldendoodle?"

"We are *not* getting a goldendoodle."

"Get a chihuahua for all I care, I'm staying. I want to see where this goes." Myles cups my cheek, sliding his hand into my hair as he kisses me. He tastes like the almond milk eggnog he had earlier—which isn't remotely close to the real thing. I still find it endearing that, despite his refusal to consume dairy, he wanted to participate in some of my family's traditions; including watching Christmas movies, spending time together by a roaring fire, matching ugly sweaters, and my dad's spiked eggnog. *Spiked is putting it lightly.*

My sister calls for us from downstairs, and we finally break apart. The three little words I've held onto for so long escape me, "I love you."

Not allowing me a chance to add a caveat, in a lightning fast movement, he rolls me onto my back and kisses me again. "Fuck, Tris, do you know how long I've waited to hear those words."

"Then, why the fuck didn't you say it first, eh?" I laugh.

"I was waiting for the right moment, I guess. I suppose now is as good a time as any. I love you, more than I've loved anyone."

"Well, now you're making it weird." I can't wipe the smile off my face. "Come on, we can't be making out like the horny kids I teach all day. We need to get downstairs."

MYLES

CHRISTMAS

Last night, Tristan and I had dinner with our parents—which included more meat than I would expect for a Christmas Eve dinner. I swear, Alberta is the Texas of Canada; I've had steak more times in the past few weeks than I have in the years since I left.

Christmas has changed for me this year. I would typically hole up in my office or apartment back home, avoiding anything that resembled holiday cheer. Being in Coal's Lake with Tristan has me merry in spite of it all. It's as if the years of hurt never existed and my only focus is on spending every other Christmas with the most amazing man I've ever known.

The snow fell all night, making it impossible for us to leave. Staying in his old room is nostalgic, but not being able to touch him was absolute torture. Waking up with my arms wrapped around him and his ass pressed against me, wanting nothing more than to slip my cock into his tight ass, or fist his cock until he's begging to fuck my mouth... It was a nightmare I never want to live again.

In matching Christmas pyjamas—and matching hard-ons—we head downstairs. It's eerily quiet. Tristan settles on the couch, roughly rubbing his face, while I make a beeline for the coffee maker. A full-size bed isn't big enough for the two of us, and he tossed and turned all night.

I spot a note on the counter next to the coffee pot:

> *Plow came through, so we are grabbing breakfast in town. We'll all be back at noon to open presents.*
> *xo, Mom*

"Tris," I call to him, holding up the note. "Everyone's gone until noon."

"Shit, what time is it?"

I check the time on the coffee pot, but in case it's off, I confirm with my phone that it's 9:23am. "Not noon." We stare at each other for a moment until we both snap, ripping off the white and blue snowflake pyjamas. "You probably shouldn't have your naked ass on the couch," I tease.

"We shouldn't have fucked in your car, my friend's bookstore, the Donner Christmas party, or every other fuckable surface in town, either."

"For the record, getting caught by 'Dudley Do-Right' was the highlight of my year."

He laughs. "We're lucky Constable Cupid let us off with a warning!"

Tristan keeps his boxer briefs on but pulls his cock out, stroking it as he keeps his eyes locked on me. I feel like an asshole fucking on his parent's couch, but I'll buy them another one tomorrow.

"Shit, I almost forgot!"

Tristan frowns. "What?"

"Your present." I rush upstairs and into Tristan's room. I meant to surprise him this morning, telling him that I want to stay. Even with it out in the open, I still wanted to do something to make him laugh.

Untangling strands of Christmas lights, I drape them haphazardly over my body. Plugging it into the battery pack, they begin twinkling. I look fucking ridiculous, but he'll love it.

I return downstairs, finding Tristan right where I left him. The second he spots me, he bursts into laughter. "Should I book you for my New Year's Eve party? I didn't know strippers covered in Christmas lights were an option."

My arms wide I turn to show off my work. Unfortunately, one of the lights snags and catches on my piercing, making me wince. "Shit!"

"What's wrong?"

"It's caught." I carefully detach it and remove the lights. "Well, that didn't go as planned."

"I fucking love you," he chuckles. "Come here."

I join him on the couch, straddling him and kissing the fuck out of the one man I've wanted my whole life, and finally have. "I love you, too."

Tristan grips my ass as I grind the length of my cock against his. He reaches between us, fisting both our cocks as I deepen our kiss. We don't have lube down here, but he coats both of us with precum as he tightens his grip. I move off him briefly to wet his cock, taking all of him in my mouth until he hits the back of my throat. It's not enough, and will hurt at first, but it's worth it to not go back upstairs.

I return on top of him, lift up and tuck my knees in, feet planted on the couch; angling myself so I can slide onto his cock. My knuckles white as I steady myself on the back of the couch. I lower myself until I take all of him. I wince at the pain that quickly turns into pleasure. He wraps his arms around me, keeping our bodies as flush as possible and I almost can't catch my breath, it feels too fucking good.

He lifts me and pushes me onto the couch, fucking me harder. His eyes are wild as he thrusts deeper. "I love you, Myles, but I'm about to fuck you like I don't."

"I'm yours. You can fuck me however the hell you want."

He thrusts hard and holds, hanging his head for a moment before his gaze returns to me. "I can't. I love the idea of it, but…"

I pull him to me by the nape of his neck and kiss him. I nip at his bottom lip and whisper, "It was always supposed to be you and me, Tris. I get it, I could never just fuck you." My ass clenches tighter around him, making him hiss. "But show me that I belong to you, how we've always belonged to each other."

Tristan continues pushing in and out of me and I savor each thrust, his fingers gripping me tight. It's never been just sex for me, and him fucking me on this couch is no different.

I meet his rhythm and pull him closer as he kisses me as if it's his last. While it should send me into a panic, I know in my heart that this incredible, sweet man is mine.

He comes hard, groaning as he fills me with every drop. Still inside me, he sits up straight and reaches for my cock. My hand covers his and I stop him.

"Pull out," I growl. His eyes widen and he slowly pulls his cock out of my ass. I stroke him a couple times, then use his cum on my hands to wet my dick. My plan to jerk myself off is tossed out the window when he swats my hand away and licks up my shaft, tugging on my balls. "Fuck," I moan, as he swirls his tongue around each of my piercings. Every time he does it, it's too much, I can't take it.

"Open for me," I command. With a satisfied smirk, his mouth falls open, ready for me, and I can't hold on any longer. Strands of cum hit his tongue and lips. He takes all of it and it has to be the hottest thing I've ever seen. He slides his tongue across my piercings as he takes all of me in his mouth, sucking every last drop from me.

When I finally catch my breath, he kisses up my body and when he reaches my mouth, I lick his lips clean and brutally kiss him. I don't give a fuck if he tastes like both of us as we explore each other's mouths and he deepens our kiss.

The front door opens and closes, we both freeze.

Shit!

Tristan scrambles off me, looking for our discarded clothes. His sister calls out from the entryway, "The roads are open, go fuck somewhere else, please."

Two sets of footsteps echo as she walks upstairs, followed by hushed voices. I'm able to make out her telling someone, "No one checks out on Christmas Day. You can be a little late."

We both let out a sigh of relief and a light chuckle. I slide on my boxer briefs and close the distance, bringing Tristan in for a slow, languid kiss. "I'm buying us a house tomorrow," I whisper into his mouth.

"Not if I don't buy one first," he counters.

With or without a goldendoodle, I'm going to spend the rest of my life with this man.

Want to know who Beth snuck into the Comet's house? Don't fret! You'll see her and the boys again in ForNever Mine, part of the Fourteen Days of Red series for Valentine's Day.

LOVED MERRY IN SPITE?

I hope you loved reading Myles and Tristan's story as much as I loved writing it!

Wherever you feel most comfortable, please consider leaving a review on Goodreads, Amazon, or social media! Your honest review means the world to me.

To keep up with all of my upcoming releases, be sure to follow me over on Amazon!

xoxo,
Irene

TWELVE DAYS OF SMUTMAS SERIES

TWELVE DAYS OF SMUTMAS

HOW THE GRINCH SAVED CHRISTINA by Amanda Bentley
GIFTING HER REVENGE by Luna Knight
FROSTED by Maia Terry
NAUGHTY ALL THE WAY by Valerie Pepper
THEIRS FOR CHRISTMAS by Effie Campbell
ALL KNOTTED UP by Elliot Ason
A COURIER FOR CHRISTMAS by Eliza Anne
SAY IT AIN'T SNOW by Bella Leigh Michaels
CUPID'S CHRISTMAS by Kelsey Woods
SINCE THERE'S NO PLACE TO GO by K.M. Gillis
MERRY IN SPITE by Irene Bahrd
A NOT SO SILENT NIGHT by J.L. Quick

ACKNOWLEDGMENTS

First, I would like to thank the amazing authors in the Twelve Days of Smutmas for putting up with me. I love you ladies so fucking much!

To my incredible friend Rachid for helping to make this story is as authentic as possible since, you know, I don't have a cock.

To my alpha readers Jodi, Bella, Kitty, and Eliza — You ladies are amazing! I'm so grateful for all of your help with this book.

To my beta readers Whisper, Flo, Lakshmi, and Amanda — Thank you for making sure everything was perfect with Tristan and Myles.

To TL Swan for writing the most perfect book boyfriend. Tristan Miles will forever be my #1.

To my incredible line editor H.M. Darling — Without you, my books would be trash! I can't thank you enough for helping make my books amazing!

Finally, thank you to all of my author friends for not letting my imposter syndrome take over, my "real life" friends for believing in me, and my family for putting up with my silly little dream of becoming a published author.

xoxo,

Irene

ABOUT THE AUTHOR

Irene Bahrd is a Gryffindor Capricorn and one of the most avid readers you'll ever meet.

She started her writing journey as a dare from a friend, after recounting dating stories from her early twenties. They inspired her to write spicy parody and romantic comedy novels that feature a variety of book boyfriends—from growly alpha heroes to cinnamon roll golden retrievers.

Her favorite genres to read include fantasy romance and contemporary dark romance. You'll find some of her favorite books and authors referenced by characters in her own books.

Irene can be found on Instagram and TikTok under @irenebahrdauthor

ALSO BY IRENE BAHRD

Love at all Cost Series

A Voice Without Reason

Not Her Villain

Unexpectedly Ruined

Top Shelf Romances Series

Mine with Extra Lime

Falling the Old Fashioned Way

Royally on the Rocks

Trouble with a Twist

Top Shelf Novella Series

Wine About It

Rosé to the Occasion

Mule Tide Cheer

Sip Happens

Stand-Alones

Never Yours

Flexible Standards

Undeclared Heir

The Al Dente Diet (Collaboration with J.L. Quick)

Pelligini Crime Daddies Parody Novella Series

Running from the Garden with Eden

Not My Bodyguard's Keeper

Thirst Trap Book Boyfriends Satire Series

Trapp Temptations: Vol. 1

Trapp Temptations: Vol. 2

Magical Mischief Parody Novella Series

Unshifted

Remaining titles to be determined

Manufactured by Amazon.ca
Acheson, AB